THE
DIARY OF
ALONZO TYPER

Fantasy & Horror Classics

By

H. P. LOVECRAFT

WITH A
DEDICATION BY
GEORGE HENRY WEISS

First published in 1938

Read & Co.

Copyright © 2020 Fantasy and Horror Classics

This edition is published by Fantasy and Horror Classics,
an imprint of Read & Co.

This book is copyright and may not be reproduced or copied in any
way without the express permission of the publisher in writing.

British Library Cataloguing-in-Publication Data
A catalogue record for this book is available
from the British Library.

Read & Co. is part of Read Books Ltd.
For more information visit
www.readandcobooks.co.uk

To
HOWARD PHILLIPS LOVECRAFT

Essayist, Poet &
Master-writer of the Weird
1890-1937

He lived—and now is dead beyond all knowing
Of life and death: the vast and formless scheme
Behind the face of nature ever showing
Has swallowed up the dreamer and the dream.
But brief the hour he had upon the stream
Of timeless time from past to future flowing
To lift his sail and catch the luminous gleam
Of stars that marked his coming and his going
Before he vanished: yet the brilliant wake
His passing left is vivid on the tide
And for the countless centuries will abide:
The genius that no death can ever take
Crowns him immortal, though a man has died.

FRANCIS FLAGG
(*George Henry Weiss*)

CONTENTS

H. P. LOVECRAFT

Howard Phillips Lovecraft was born in 1890 in Rhode Island, USA. Although a sickly boy, Lovecraft began writing at a very young age, quickly developing a deep and abiding interest in science. At just sixteen he was writing a monthly astronomy column for his local newspaper. However, in 1908, Lovecraft suffered a nervous breakdown and failed to get into university, sparking a period of five years in which he all but vanished.

In 1913, Lovecraft was invited to join the UAPA (United Amateur Press Association)—a development which re-invigorated his writing. In 1917, he began to focus on fiction, producing such well-known early stories as *Dagon* and *A Reminiscence of Dr. Samuel Johnson*. In 1924, Lovecraft married and moved to New York, but he disliked life there intensely, and struggled to find work. A few years later, penniless and now divorced, he returned to Rhode Island. It was here, during the last decade of his life, that Lovecraft produced the vast majority of his best-known fiction, including *The Dunwich Horror*, *The Shadow over Innsmouth*, *The Thing on the Doorstep* and arguably his most famous story, *The Call of Cthulhu*. Having suffered from cancer of the small intestine for more than a year, Lovecraft died in March of 1937.

THE DIARY
OF ALONZO TYPER

EDITOR'S NOTE: Alonzo Hasbrouck Typer of Kingston, New York, was last seen and recognised on April 17, 1908, around noon, at the Hotel Richmond in Batavia. He was the only survivor of an ancient Ulster County family, and was fifty-three years old at the time of his disappearance.

Mr Typer was educated privately and at Columbia and Heidelberg universities. All his life was spent as a student, the field of his researches including many obscure and generally feared borderlands of human knowledge. His papers on vampirism, ghouls, and poltergeist phenomena were privately printed after rejection by many publishers. He resigned from the Society for Psychical Research in 1920 after a series of peculiarly bitter controversies.

At various times Mr Typer travelled extensively, sometimes dropping out of sight for long periods. He is known to have visited obscure spots in Nepal, India, Tibet, and Indo-China, and passed most of the year 1899 on mysterious Easter Island. The extensive search for Mr Typer after his disappearance yielded no results, and his estate was divided among distant cousins in New York City.

The diary herewith presented was allegedly found in the ruins of a large country house near Attica, N.Y., which had borne a curiously sinister reputation for generations before its collapse. The edifice was very old, antedating the general white settlement of the region, and had formed the home of a strange and secretive family named van der Heyl, which had migrated from Albany in 1746 under a curious cloud of witchcraft suspicion.

The structure probably dated from about 1760.

Of the history of the van der Heyls very little is known. They remained entirely aloof from their normal neighbours, employed negro servants brought directly from Africa and speaking little English, and educated their children privately and at European colleges. Those of them who went out into the world were soon lost to sight, though not before gaining evil repute for association with Black Mass groups and cults of even darker significance.

Around the dreaded house a straggling village arose, populated by Indians and later by renegades from the surrounding country, which bore the dubious name of Chorazin. Of the singular hereditary strains which afterwards appeared in the mixed Chorazin villagers, several monographs have been written by ethnologists. Just behind the village, and in sight of the van der Heyl house, is a steep hill crowned with a peculiar ring of ancient standing stones which the Iroquois always regarded with fear and loathing. The origin and nature of the stones, whose date, according to archaeological and climatological evidence, must be fabulously early, is a problem still unsolved.

From about 1795 onward, the legends of the incoming pioneers and later population have much to say about strange cries and chants proceeding at certain seasons from Chorazin and from the great house and hill of standing stones; though there is reason to suppose that the noises ceased about 1872, when the entire van der Heyl household—servants and all— suddenly and simultaneously disappeared.

Thenceforward the house was deserted; for other disastrous events—including three unexplained deaths, five disappearances, and four cases of sudden insanity—occurred when later owners and interested visitors attempted to stay in it. The house, village, and extensive rural areas on all sides reverted to the state and were auctioned off in the absence of discoverable van der Heyl heirs. Since about 1890 the owners (successively the late Charles A. Shields and his son Oscar S. Shields, of Buffalo) have left the entire property in a state of absolute neglect, and have warned all inquirers not to visit the region.

Of those known to have approached the house during the last forty years, most were occult students, police officers, newspaper men, and odd characters from abroad. Among the latter was a mysterious Eurasian, probably from Cochin-China, whose later appearance with blank mind and bizarre mutilations excited wide press notice in 1903.

Mr Typer's diary—a book about 6 by 3 1/2 inches in size, with tough paper and an oddly durable binding of thin sheet metal—was discovered in the possession of one of the decadent Chorazin villagers on November 16, 1935, by a state policemen sent to investigate the rumoured collapse of the deserted van der Heyl mansion. The house had indeed fallen, obviously from sheer age and decrepitude, in the severe gale of November 12. Disintegration was peculiarly complete, and no thorough search of the ruins could be made for several weeks. John Eagle, the swarthy, simian-faced, Indian-like villager who had the diary, said that he found the book quite near the surface of the debris, in what must have been an upper front room.

Very little of the contents of the house could be identified, though an enormous and astonishingly solid brick vault in the cellar (whose ancient iron door had to be blasted open because of the strangely figured and perversely tenacious lock) remained intact and presented several puzzling features. For one thing, the walls were covered with still undeciphered hieroglyphs roughly incised in the brickwork. Another peculiarity was a huge circular aperture in the rear of the vault, blocked by a cave-in evidently caused by the collapse of the house.

But strangest of all was the apparently *recent* deposit of some fetid, slimy, pitch-black substance on the flagstoned floor, extending in a yard-board, irregular line with one end at the blocked circular aperture. Those who first opened the vault declared that the place smelled like the snake-house at a zoo.

The diary, which was apparently designed solely to cover an investigation of the dreaded van der Heyl house by the vanished Mr Typer, has been proved by handwriting experts to be genuine. The script shows signs of increasing nervous strain as it progresses towards the end, in places becoming almost illegible. Chorazin villagers—whose stupidity and taciturnity baffle all students of the region and its secrets—admit no recollection of Mr Typer as distinguished from other rash visitors to the dreaded house.

The text of the diary is here given verbatim and without comment. How to interpret it, and what, other than the writer's madness, to infer from it, the reader must decide for himself. Only the future can tell what its value may be in solving a generation-old mystery. It may be remarked that genealogists confirm Mr Typer's belated memory in the matter of *Adriaen Sleght.*

THE DIARY

April 17, 1908

Arrived here about 6 p.m. Had to walk all the way from Attica in the teeth of an oncoming storm, for no one would rent me a horse or rig, and I can't run an automobile. This place is even worse than I had expected, and I dread what is coming, even though I long at the same time to learn the secret. All too soon will come the night—the old Walpurgis Sabbat horror—and after that time in Wales I know what to look for. Whatever comes, I shall not flinch. Prodded by some unfathomable urge, I have given my whole life to the quest of unholy mysteries. I came here for nothing else, and will not quarrel with fate.

It was very dark when I got here, though the sun had by no means set. The storm-clouds were the densest I had ever seen, and I could not have found my way but for the lightning-flashes. The village is a hateful little backwater, and its few inhabitants no better than idiots. One of them saluted me in a queer way, as if he knew men. I could see very little of the landscape— just a small, swampy valley of strange brown weed-stalks and dead fungi surrounded by scraggly, evilly twisted trees with bare boughs. But behind the village is a dismal-looking hill on whose summit is a circle of great stones with another stone at the centre. That, without question, is the vile primordial thing V——told me about at the N——Sabbat.

The great house lies in the midst of a park all overgrown with curious-looking briars. I could scarcely break through, and when I did the vast age and decrepitude of the building almost stopped me from entering. The place looked filthy and diseased, and I wondered how so leprous a bulk could hang together. It is wooden; and though its original lines are hidden by a bewildering tangle of wings added at various dates, I think it was first built in the square colonial fashion of New England. Probably that was easier to build than a Dutch stone house— and then, too, I recall that Dirck van der Heyl's wife was from Salem, a daughter of the unmentionable Abaddon Corey. There was a small pillared porch, and I got under it just as the storm burst. It was a fiendish tempest—black as midnight, with rain in sheets, thunder and lightning like the day of general dissolution, and a wind that actually clawed at me.

The door was unlocked, so I took out my electric torch and went inside. Dust was inches deep on floor and furniture, and the place smelled like a mould-caked tomb. There was a hall reaching all the way through, and a curving staircase on the right.

I ploughed my way upstairs and selected this front room to camp out in. The whole place seems fully furnished, though most of the furniture is breaking down. This is written at eight o'clock, after a cold meal from my travelling-case. After this the village people will bring me supplies; though they won't agree to come any closer than the ruins of the park gate until (as they say) later. I wish I could get rid of an unpleasant feeling of familiarity with this place.

Later

I am conscious of several presences in this house. One in particular is decidedly hostile towards me—a malevolent will which is seeking to break down my own and overcome me. I must not countenance this for an instant, but must use all my forces to resist it. It is appallingly evil, and definitely non-human. I think it must be allied to powers outside Earth—powers in the spaces behind time and beyond the universe. It towers like a colossus, bearing out what is said in the Aklo writings. There is such a feeling of vast size connected with it that I wonder these chambers can contain its bulk—and yet it has no visible bulk. Its age must be unutterably vast—shockingly, indescribably so.

April 18

Slept very little last night. At 3 a.m. a strange, creeping wind began to pervade the whole region, ever rising until the house rocked as if in a typhoon. As I went down the staircase to see to the rattling front door the darkness took half-visible forms in my imagination. Just below the landing I was pushed violently from behind—by the wind, I suppose, though I could have sworn I saw the dissolving outlines of a gigantic black paw as I turned quickly about. I did not lose my footing, but safely finished the descent and shot the heavy bolt of the dangerously shaking door.

I had not meant to explore the house before dawn; yet now, unable to sleep again and fired with mixed terror and curiosity. I felt reluctant to postpone my search. With my powerful torch I ploughed through the dust to the great south parlour, where I knew the portraits would be. There they were, just as V——

had said, and as I seemed to know from some obscurer source as well. Some were so blackened and dust-clouded that I could make little or nothing of them, but from those I could trace I recognised that they were indeed of the hateful line of the van der Heyls. Some of the paintings seemed to suggest faces I had known; but just what faces, I could not recall.

The outlines of that frightful hybrid Joris—spawned in 1773 by old Dirck's youngest daughter—were clearest of all, and I could trace the green eyes and the serpent look in his face. Every time I shut off the flashlight that face would seem to glow in the dark until I half fancied it shone with a faint, greenish light of its own. The more I looked, the more evil it seemed, and I turned away to avoid hallucinations of changing expression.

But that to which I turned was even worse. The long, dour face, small, closely set eyes and swine-like features identified it at once, even though the artist had striven to make the snout look as human as possible. This was what V——had whispered about. As I stared in horror, I thought the eyes took on a reddish glow, and for a moment the background seemed replaced by an alien and seemingly irrelevant scene—a lone, bleak moor beneath a dirty yellow sky, whereon grew a wretched-looking blackthorn bush. Fearing for my sanity, I rushed from that accursed gallery to the dust-cleared corner upstairs where I have my "camp".

Later

Decided to explore some of the labyrinthine wings of the house by daylight. I cannot get lost, for my footprints are distinct in the ankle-deep dust, and I can trace other identifying marks when necessary. It is curious how easily I learn the intricate windings of the corridors. Followed a long, outflung northerly "ell" to its extremity, and came to a locked door, which I forced. Beyond was a very small room quite crowded with furniture, and with the panelling badly worm-eaten. On the outer wall I spied a black space behind the rotting woodwork, and discovered a narrow secret passage leading downwards to unknown inky depths. It was a steeply inclined chute or tunnel without steps or hand-holds, and I wondered what its use could have been.

Above the fireplace was a mouldy painting, which I found on close inspection to be that of a young woman in the dress of the late eighteenth century. The face is of classic beauty, yet with the most fiendishly evil expression which I have ever known the human countenance to bear. Not merely callousness, greed, and cruelty, but some quality hideous beyond human comprehension seems to sit upon those finely carved features. And as I looked it seemed to me that the artist—or the slow processes of mould and decay—had imparted to that pallid complexion a sickly greenish cast, and the least suggestion of an almost imperceptibly scaly texture. Later I ascended to the attic, where I found several chests of strange books—many of utterly alien aspects in letters and in physical form alike. One contained variants of the Aklo formulae which I had never known to exist. I have not yet examined the books on the dusty shelves downstairs.

April 19

There are certainly unseen presences here, even though the dust bears no footprints but my own. Cut a path through the briars yesterday to the park gate where my supplies are left, but this morning I found it closed. Very odd, since the bushes are barely stirring with sprang sap. Again I have that feeling of something at hand so colossal that the chambers can scarcely contain it. This time I feel that more than one of the presences is of such a size, and I know now that the third Aklo ritual— which I found in that book in the attic yesterday—would make such beings solid and visible. Whether I shall dare to try this materialisation remains to be seen. The perils are great.

Last night I began to glimpse evanescent shadow-faces and forms in the dim corners of the halls and chambers—faces and forms so hideous and loathsome that I dare not describe them. They seem allied in substance to that titanic paw which tried to push me down the stairs the night before last, and must of course be phantoms of my disturbed imagination. What I am seeking would not be quite like these things. I have seen the paw again, sometimes alone and sometimes with its mate, but I have resolved to ignore all such phenomena.

Early this afternoon I explored the cellar for the first time, descending by a ladder found in a store-room, since the wooden steps had rotted away. The whole place is a mass of nitrous encrustations with amorphous mounds marking the spots where various objects have disintegrated. At the farther end is a narrow passage which seems to extend under the northerly "ell" where I found the little locked room, and at the end of this is a heavy brick wall with a locked iron door. Apparently belonging to a vault of some sort, this wall and door bear evidences of eighteenth-century workmanship and must be contemporary with the oldest additions to the house—clearly pre-Revolutionary. On the lock, which is obviously older than the rest of the ironwork, are engraved certain symbols which I cannot decipher.

V——had not told me about this vault. It fills me with a greater disquiet than anything else I have seen, for every time I approach it I have an almost irresistible impulse to *listen* for something. Hitherto no untoward *sounds* have marked my stay in this malign place. As I left the cellar I wished devoutly that the steps were still there; for my progress up the ladder seemed maddeningly slow. I do not want to go down there again—and yet some evil genius urges me to try it *at night* if I would learn what is to be learned.

April 20

I have sounded the depths of horror—only to be made aware of still lower depths. Last night the temptation was too strong, and in the black small hours I descended once more into that nitrous hellish cellar with my flashlight, tiptoeing among the amorphous heaps to that terrible brick wall and locked door. I made no sound, and refrained from whispering any of the incantations I knew, but I listened with mad intentness.

At last I heard the sounds from beyond those barred plates of sheet iron, the menacing padding and muttering, as of gigantic night-things within. Then, too, there was a damnable slithering, as of a vast serpent or sea-beast dragging its monstrous folds over a paved floor. Nearly paralysed with fright, I glanced at the huge rusty lock, and at the alien, cryptic hieroglyphs graven upon it. They were signs I could not recognise, and something in their vaguely Mongoloid technique hinted at a blasphemous and indescribable antiquity. At times I fancied I could see them glowing with a greenish light.

I turned to flee, but found that vision of the titan paws before me, the great talons seeming to swell and become more tangible as I gazed. Out of the cellar's evil blackness they stretched, with shadowy hints of scaly wrists beyond them, and with a waxing, malignant will guiding their horrible gropings. Then I heard from behind me—within that abominable vault—a fresh burst of muffled reverberations which seemed to echo from far horizons like distant thunder. Impelled by this greater fear, I advanced towards the shadowy paws with my flashlight and saw them vanish before the full force of the electric beam. Then up the ladder I raced, torch between my teeth, nor did I rest till I had regained my upstairs "camp".

What is to be my ultimate end, I dare not imagine. I came as a seeker, but now I know that something is seeking me. I could not leave if I wished. This morning I tried to go to the gate for my supplies, but found the briars twisted tightly in my path. It was the same in every direction—behind and on all sides of the house. In places the brown, barbed vines had uncurled to astonishing heights, forming a steel-like hedge against my egress. The villagers are connected with all this. When I went indoors I found my supplies in the great front hall, though without any clue to how they came there. I am sorry now that I swept the dust away. I shall scatter some more and see what prints are left.

This afternoon I read some of the books in the great shadowy library at the rear of the ground floor, and formed certain suspicions which I cannot bear to mention. I had never seen the text of the Pnakotic Manuscripts or of the Eltdown Shards before, and would not have come here had I known what they contain. I believe it is too late now—for the awful Sabbat is only ten days away. It is for that night of horror that *they* are saving me.

April 21

I have been studying the portraits again. Some have names attached and I noticed one—of an evil-faced woman, painted some two centuries ago—which puzzled me. It bore the name of Trintje van der Heyl Slegth, and I have a distinct impression that I once met the name of Sleght before, in some significant connection. It was not horrible then, though it becomes so now. I must rack my brain for the clue.

The eyes of these pictures haunt me. Is it possible that some of them are emerging more distinctly from their shrouds of dust and decay and mould? The serpent-faced and swine-faced warlocks stare horribly at me from their blackened frames, and a score of other hybrid faces are beginning to peer out of shadowy backgrounds. There is a hideous look of family resemblance in them all, and that which is human is more horrible than that which is non-human. I wish they reminded me less of other faces—faces I have known in the past. They were an accursed line, and Cornelis of Leyden was the worst of them. It was *he* who broke down the barrier after his father had found that other key. I am sure that V——knows only a fragment of the horrible truth, so that I am indeed unprepared and defenceless. What of the line before old Claes? What he did in 1591 could never have been done without generations of evil heritage, or some link with the outside. And what of the branches this monstrous line has sent forth? Are they scattered over the world, all awaiting their common heritage of horror? I must recall the place where I once so particularly noticed the name of Sleght.

I wish I could be sure that these pictures stay always in their frames. For several hours now I have been seeing momentary presences like the earlier paws and shadow-faces and forms, but closely duplicating some of the ancient portraits. Somehow I can never glimpse a presence and the portrait it resembles at the same time—the light is always wrong for one or the other, or else the presence and the portrait are in different rooms.

Perhaps, as I have hoped, the presences are mere figments of imagination, but I cannot be sure now. Some are female, and of the same hellish beauty as the picture in the little locked room. Some are like no portrait I have seen, yet make me feel that their painted features lurk unrecognised beneath the mould and soot of canvases I cannot decipher. A few, I desperately fear, have approached materialisation in solid or semi-solid form—and some have a dreadful and unexplained familiarity.

There is one woman who in fell loveliness excels all the rest. Her poisonous charms are like a honeyed flower growing on the brink of hell. When I look at her closely she vanishes, only to reappear later. Her face has a greenish cast, and now and then I fancy I can spy a suspicion of the squamous in its smooth texture. Who is she? Is she that being who must have dwelt in the little locked room a century and more ago?

My supplies were again left in the front hall—that, clearly, is to be the custom. I had sprinkled dust about to catch footprints, but this morning the whole hall was swept clean by some unknown agency.

April 22

This has been a day of horrible discovery. I explored the cobwebbed attic again, and found a carved, crumbling chest—plainly from Holland—full of blasphemous books and papers far older than any hitherto encountered here. There was a Greek *Necronomicon*, a Norman-French *Livre d'Eibon*, and a first edition of old Ludvig Prinn's *De Vermis Mysteriis*. But the old bound manuscript was the worst. It was in low Latin, and full of the strange, crabbed handwriting of Claes van der Heyl, being evidently the diary or notebook kept by him between 1560 and 1580. When I unfastened the blackened silver clasp and opened the yellowed leaves a coloured drawing fluttered out—the likeness of a monstrous creature resembling nothing so much as a squid, beaked and tentacled, with great yellow eyes, and with certain abominable approximations to the human form in its contours.

I had never before seen so utterly loathsome and nightmarish a form. On the paws, feet, and head-tentacles were curious claws—reminding me of the colossal shadow-shapes which had groped so horribly in my path—while the entity as a whole sat upon a great throne-like pedestal inscribed with unknown hieroglyphs of vaguely Chinese cast. About both writing and image there hung an air of sinister evil so profound and pervasive that I could not think it the product of any one world or age. Rather must that monstrous shape be a focus for all the evil in unbounded space, throughout the eons past and to come—and those elditch symbols be vile sentient ikons endowed with a morbid life of their own and ready to wrest themselves from the parchment for the reader's destruction. To the meaning of that monster and of those hieroglyphs I had no clue, but I knew that both had been traced with a hellish precision and for no nameable purpose. As I studied the leering characters, their kinship to the symbols on that ominous lock in the cellar became more and more manifest. I left the picture in the attic, for never could sleep come to me with such a thing near by.

All the afternoon and evening I read in the manuscript book of old Claes van der Heyl; and what I read will cloud and make horrible whatever period of life lies ahead of me. The genesis of the world and of previous worlds, unfolded itself before my eyes. I learned of the city Shamballah, built by the Lemurians fifty million years ago, yet inviolate still behind its walls of psychic force in the eastern desert. I learned of the Book of Dzyan, whose first six chapters antedate the Earth, and which was old when the lords of Venus came through space in their ships to civilise our planet. And I saw recorded in writing for the first time that name which others had spoken to me in whispers, and which I had known in a closer and more horrible way—the shunned and dreaded name of *Yian-Ho*.

In several places I was held up by passages requiring a key. Eventually, from various allusions, I gathered that old Claes had not dared to embody all his knowledge in one book, but had left certain points for another. Neither volume can be wholly intelligible without its fellow; hence I have resolved to find the second one if it lies anywhere within this accursed house. Though plainly a prisoner, I have not lost my lifelong zeal for the unknown; and am determined to probe the cosmos as deeply as possible before doom comes.

April 23

Searched all the morning for the second diary, and found it about noon in a desk in the little locked room. Like the first, it is in Claes van der Heyl's barbarous Latin, and it seems to consist of disjointed notes referring to various sections of the other. Glancing through the leaves, I spied at once the abhorred name of Yian-Ho—of Yian-Ho, that lost and hidden city wherein brood eon-old secrets, and of which dim memories older than the body lurk behind the minds of all men. It was repeated many times, and the text around it was strewn with crudely drawn hieroglyphs plainly akin to those on the pedestal in that hellish drawing I had seen. Here, clearly, lay the key to that monstrous tentacled shape and its forbidden message. With this knowledge I ascended the creaking stairs to the attic of cobwebs and horror. When I tried to open the attic door it stuck as never before. Several times it resisted every effort to open it, and when at last it gave way I had a distinct feeling that some colossal, unseen shape had suddenly released it—a shape that soared away on non-material but audibly beating wings. When I found the horrible drawing I felt that it was not precisely where I had left it. Applying the key in the other book, I soon saw that the latter was no instant guide to the secret. It was only a clue—a clue to a secret too black to be left lightly guarded. It would take hours— perhaps days—to extract the awful message.

Shall I live long enough to learn the secret? The shadowy black arms and paws haunt my vision more and more now, and seem even more titanic than at first. Nor am I ever long free from those vague, unhuman presences whose nebulous bulk seems too vast for the chambers to contain. And now and then the grotesque, evanescent faces and forms, and the mocking portrait-shapes, troop before me in bewildering confusion.

Truly, there are terrible primal arcana of Earth which had better be left unknown and unevoked; dread secrets which have nothing to do with man, and which man may learn only in exchange for peace and sanity; cryptic truths which make the knower evermore an alien among his kind, and cause him to walk alone on Earth. Likewise are there dread survivals of things older and more potent than man; things that have blasphemously straggled down through the eons to ages never meant for them; monstrous entities that have lain sleeping endlessly in incredible crypts and remote caverns, outside the laws of reason and causation, and ready to be waked by such blasphemers as shall know their dark forbidden signs and furtive passwords.

April 24

Studied the picture and the key all day in the attic. At sunset I heard strange sounds, of a sort not encountered before and seeming to come from far away. Listening, I realised that they must flow from that queer abrupt hill with the circle of standing stones, which lies behind the village and some distance north of the house. I had heard that there was a path from the house leading up that hill to the primal cromlech, and had suspected that at certain seasons the van der Heyls had much occasion to use it; but the whole matter had hitherto lain latent in my consciousness. The present sounds consisted of a shrill piping intermingled with a peculiar and hideous sort of hissing or whistling, a bizarre, alien kind of music, like nothing which the annals of Earth describe. It was very faint, and soon faded, but the matter has set me thinking. It is towards the hill that the long, northerly "ell" with the secret chute, and the locked brick vault under it, extend. Can there be any connection which has so far eluded me?

April 25

I have made a peculiar and disturbing discovery about the nature of my imprisonment. Drawn towards the hill by a sinister fascination, I found the briars giving way before me, *but in that direction only.* There is a ruined gate, and beneath the bushes the traces of an old path no doubt exist. The briars extend part-way up and all around the hill, though the summit with the standing stones bears only a curious growth of moss and stunted grass. I climbed the hill and spent several hours there, noticing a strange wind which seems always to sweep around the forbidding monoliths and which sometimes seems to whisper in an oddly articulate though darkly cryptic fashion.

These stones, both in colour and in texture, resemble nothing I have seen elsewhere. They are neither brown nor grey, but rather of a dirty yellow merging into an evil green and having a suggestion of chameleon-like variability. Their texture is queerly like that of a scaled serpent, and is inexplicably nauseous to the touch—being as cold and clammy as the skin of a toad or other reptile. Near the central menhir is a singular stone-rimmed hollow which I cannot explain, but which may possibly form the entrance to a long-choked well or tunnel. When I sought to descend the hill at points away from the house I found the briars intercepting me as before, though the path towards the house was easily retraceable.

April 26

Up on the hill again this evening, and found that windy whispering much more distinct. The almost angry humming came close to actual speech, of a vague, sibilant sort, and reminded me of the strange piping chant I had heard from afar. After sunset there came a curious flash of premature summer lightning on the northern horizon, followed almost at once by a queer detonation high in the fading sky. Something about this phenomenon disturbed me greatly, and I could not escape the impression that the noise ended in a kind of unhuman hissing speech which trailed off into guttural cosmic laughter. Is my mind tottering at last, or has my unwarranted curiosity evoked unheard-of horrors from the twilight spaces? The Sabbat is close at hand now. What will be the end?

April 27

At last my dreams are to be realised! Whether or not my life or spirit or body will be claimed, I shall enter the gateway! Progress in deciphering those crucial hieroglyphs in the picture has been slow, but this afternoon I hit upon the final clue. By evening I knew their meaning—and that meaning can apply in only one way to the things I have encountered in this house.

25

There is beneath this house—sepulchered I know not where—an ancient forgotten One Who will show me the gateway I would enter, and give me the lost signs and words I shall need. How long it has lain buried here, forgotten save by those who reared the stones on the hill, and by those who later sought out this place and built this house, I cannot conjecture. It was in search of this Thing, beyond question, that Hendrik van der Heyl came to New-Netherland in 1638. Men of this Earth know It not, save in the secret whispers of the fear-shaken few who have found or inherited the key. No human eye has even yet glimpsed It—unless, perhaps, the vanished wizards of this house delved further than has been guessed.

With knowledge of the symbols came likewise a mastery of the Seven Lost Signs of Terror, and a tacit recognition of the hideous and unutterable Words of Fear. All that remains for me to accomplish is the Chant which will transfigure that Forgotten One Who is Guardian of the Ancient Gateway. I marvel much at the Chant. It is composed of strange and repellent gutturals and disturbing sibilants resembling no language I have ever encountered, even in the blackest chapters of the *Livre d'Eibon*. When I visited the hill at sunset I tried to read it aloud, but evoked in response only a vague, sinister fumbling on the far horizon, and a thin cloud of elemental dust that writhed and whirled like some evil living thing. Perhaps I do not pronounce the alien syllables correctly, or perhaps it is only on the Sabbat—that hellish Sabbat for which the Powers in this house are without question holding me—that the great Transfiguration can occur.

Had an odd spell of fright this morning. I thought for a moment that I recalled where I had seen that baffling name of Sleght before, and the prospect of realisation filled me with unutterable horror.

April 28

Today dark ominous clouds have hovered intermittently over the circle on the hill. I have noticed such clouds several times before, but their contours and arrangements now hold a fresh significance. They are snake-like and fantastic, and curiously like the evil shadow-shapes I have seen in the house. They float in a circle around the primal cromlech, revolving repeatedly as though endowed with a sinister life and purpose. I could swear that they give forth an angry murmuring. After some fifteen minutes they sail slowly away, ever to the eastward, like the units of a straggling battalion. Are they indeed those dread Ones whom Solomon knew of old—those giant black beings whose number is legion and whose tread doth shake the earth?

I have been rehearsing the Chant that will transfigure the Nameless Thing; yet strange fears assail me even when I utter the syllables under my breath. Piecing all evidence together, I have now discovered that the only way to It is through the locked cellar vault. That vault was built with a hellish purpose, and must cover the hidden burrow leading to the Immemorial Lair. What guardians live endlessly within, flourishing from century to century on an unknown nourishment, only the mad may conjecture. The warlocks of this house, who called them out of inner Earth, have known them only too well, as the shocking portraits and memories of the place reveal.

What troubles me most is the limited nature of the Chant. It evokes the Nameless One, yet provides no method for the control of That Which is evoked. There are, of course, the general signs and gestures, but whether they will prove effective towards such a One remains to be seen. Still, the rewards are great enough to justify any danger, and I could not retreat if I would, since an unknown force plainly urges me on.

I have discovered one more obstacle. Since the locked cellar vault must be traversed, the key to that place must be found. The lock is far too strong for forcing. That the key is somewhere hereabouts cannot be doubted, but the time before the Sabbat is very short. I must search diligently and thoroughly. It will take courage to unlock that iron door, for what prisoned horrors may not lurk within?

Later

I have been shunning the cellar for the past day or two, but late this afternoon I again descended to those forbidding precincts.

At first all was silent, but within five minutes the menacing padding and muttering began once more beyond the iron door. This time it was louder and more terrifying than on any previous occasion, and I likewise recognised the slithering that bespoke some monstrous sea-beast—now swifter and nervously intensified, as if the thing were striving to force its way through the portal to where I stood.

As the pacing grew louder, more restless, and more sinister, there began to pound through it those hellish and unidentifiable reverberations which I had heard on my second visit to the cellar—those muffled reverberations which seemed to echo from far horizons like distant thunder. Now, however, their volume was magnified a hundredfold, and their timbre freighted with new and terrifying implications. I can compare the sound to nothing more aptly than to the roar of some dread monster of the vanished saurian age, when primal horrors roamed the Earth, and Valusia's serpent-men laid the foundation-stones of evil magic. To such a roar—but swelled to deafening heights reached by no known organic throat—was this shocking sound akin. Dare I unlock the door and face the onslaught of what lies beyond?

April 29

The key to the vault is found. I came upon it this noon in the little locked room—buried beneath rubbish in a drawer of the ancient desk, as if some belated effort to conceal it had been made. It was wrapped in a crumbling newspaper dated October 31, 1872; but there was an inner wrapping of dried skin—evidently the hide of some unknown reptile—which bore a Low Latin message in the same crabbed writing as that of the notebooks I found. As I had thought, the lock and key were vastly older than the vault. Old Claes van der Heyl had had them ready for something he or his descendants meant to do— and how much older than he they were I could not estimate. Deciphering the Latin message, I trembled in a fresh access of clutching terror and nameless awe.

"The secrets of the monstrous primal Ones," ran the crabbed text, "whose cryptic words relate the hidden things that were before man; the things no one of Earth should learn, lest peace be for ever forfeited; shall by me never suffer revelation. To Yian-Ho, that lost and forbidden city of countless eons whose place may not be told, I have been in the veritable flesh of this body, as none other among the living has been. Therein have I found, and thence have I borne away, that knowledge which I would gladly lose, though I may not. I have learnt to bridge a gap that should not be bridged, and must call out of the Earth That Which should not be waked nor called. And what is sent to follow me will not sleep till I or those after me have found and done what is to be found and done.

"That which I have awaked and borne away with me, I may not part with again. So is it written in the Book of Hidden Things. That which I have willed to be has twined its dreadful shape around me, and—if I live not to do the bidding—around those children born and unborn who shall come after me, until the bidding be done. Strange may be their joinings, and awful the aid they may summon till the end be reached. Into lands unknown and dim must they seeking go, and a house must be built for the outer guardians.

"This is the key to that lock which was given me in the dreadful, eon-old and forbidden city of Yian-Ho; the lock which I or mine must place upon the vestibule of That Which is to be found. And may the Lord of Yaddith succour me—or him—who must set that lock in place or turn the key thereof."

Such was the message—a message which, once I had read it, I seemed to have known before. Now, as I write these words, the key is before me. I gaze on it with mixed dread and longing, and cannot find words to describe its aspect. It is of the same unknown, subtly greenish frosted metal as the lock; a metal best compared to brass tarnished with verdigris. Its design is alien and fantastic, and the coffin-shaped end of the ponderous bulk leaves no doubt of the lock it was meant to fit. The handle roughly forms a strange, non-human image, whose exact outlines and identity cannot now be traced. Upon holding it for any length of time I seem to feel an alien, anomalous life in the cold metal—a quickening or pulsing too feeble for ordinary recognition.

Below the eidolon is graven a faint, eon-worn legend in those blasphemous, Chinese-like hieroglyphs I have come to know so well. I can make out only the beginning—the words: "My vengeance lurks . . ."—before the text fades to indistinctness. There is some fatality in this timely finding of the key—for tomorrow night comes the hellish Sabbat. But strangely enough, amidst all this hideous expectancy, that question of the Sleght name bothers me more and more. Why should I dread to find it linked with the van der Heyls?

Walpurgis-Eve—April 30

The time has come. I waked last night to see the key glowing with a lurid greenish radiance—that same morbid green which I have seen in the eyes and skin of certain portraits here, on the shocking lock and key, on the monstrous menhirs of the hill, and in a thousand other recesses of my consciousness. There were strident whispers in the air—sibilant whistlings like those of the wind around that dreadful cromlech. Something spoke to me out of the frore aether of space, and it said, "The hour falls." It is an omen, and I laugh at my own fears. Have I not the dread words and the Seven Lost Signs of Terror—the power coercive of any Dweller in the cosmos or in the unknown darkened spaces? I will no longer hesitate.

The heavens are very dark, as if a terrific storm were coming on—a storm even greater than that of the night when I reached here, nearly a fortnight ago. From the village, less than a mile away, I hear a queer and unwonted babbling. It is as I thought—these poor degraded idiots are within the secret, and keep the awful Sabbat on the hill.

Here in the house the shadows gather densely. In the darkness the sky before me almost glows with a greenish light of its own. I have not yet been to the cellar. It is better that I wait, lest the sound of that muttering and padding—those slitherings and muffled reverberations—unnerve me before I can unlock the fateful door.

Of what I shall encounter, and what I must do, I have only the most general idea. Shall I find my task in the vault itself, or must I burrow deeper into the nighted heart of our planet? There are things I do not yet understand—or at least, prefer not to understand—despite a dreadful, increasing, and inexplicable sense of bygone familiarity with this fearsome house. That chute, for instance, leading down from the little locked room. But I think I know why the wing with the vault extends towards the hill.

6 p.m.

Looking out of the north windows, I can see a group of villagers on the hill. They seem unaware of the lowering sky, and are digging near the great central menhir. It occurs to me that they are working on that stone-rimmed hollow place which looks like a long-choked tunnel entrance. What is to come? How much of the olden Sabbat rites have these people retained? That key glows horribly—it is not imagination. Dare I use it as it must be used? Another matter has greatly disturbed me. Glancing nervously through a book in the library I cam upon an ampler form of the name that has teased my memory so sorely: "Trintje, wife of Adriaen Sleght." The *Adriaen* leads me to the very brink of recollection.

Midnight

Horror is unleashed, but I must not weaken. The storm has broken with pandemoniac fury, and lightning has struck the hill three times, yet the hybrid, malformed villagers are gathering within the cromlech. I can see them in the almost constant flashes. The great standing stones loom up shockingly, and have a dull green luminosity that reveals them even when the lightning is not there. The peals of the thunder are deafening, and every one seems to be horribly *answered* from some indeterminate direction. As I write, the creatures on the hill have begun to chant and howl and scream in a degraded, half-simian version of the ancient ritual. Rain pours down like a flood, yet they leap and emit sounds in a kind of diabolic ecstasy.

"*Ia, Shub-Niggurath! The Goat with a Thousand Young!*"

But the worst thing is within the house. Even at this height, I have begun to hear sounds from the cellar. *It is the padding and muttering and slithering and muffled reverberations within the vault....*

Memories come and go. That name of *Adriaen Sleght* pounds

oddly at my consciousness. Dirck van der Heyl's son-in-law . . .
his child old Dirck's granddaughter and Abaddon Corey's great-
granddaughter. . . .

Later

Merciful God! *At last I know where I saw that name.* I know,
and am transfixed with horror. All is lost. . . .
The key has begun to feel warm as my left hand nervously
clutches it. At times that vague quickening or pulsing is so
distinct that I can almost feel the living metal move. It came
from Yian-Ho for a terrible purpose, and to me—who all too
late know the thin stream of van der Heyl blood that trickles
down through the Sleghts into my own lineage—has descended
the hideous task of fulfilling that purpose. . . .
My courage and curiosity wane. I know the horror that lies
beyond that iron door. What if Claes van der Heyl was my
ancestor—need I expiate his nameless sin? *I will not—I swear I
will not!* . . . (the writing here grows indistinct) . . . too late—
cannot help self-black paws materialise—am dragged away
towards the cellar. . . .

Printed in Great Britain
by Amazon